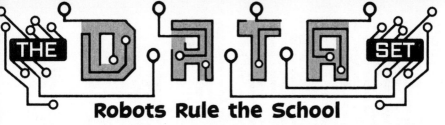

DANGER! ACTION! TROUBLE! ADVENTURE!

THE D A T A SET

Robots Rule the School

By Ada Hopper   Illustrated by Sam Ricks

LITTLE SIMON
New York London Toronto Sydney New Delhi

LITTLE SIMON

An imprint of Simon & Schuster Children's Publishing Division

1230 Avenue of the Americas, New York, New York 10020

First Little Simon hardcover edition July 2016 • Copyright © 2016 by Simon & Schuster, Inc.

Designed by John Daly. The text of this book was set in Serifa.

Manufactured in the United States of America 0516 OFF 10 9 8 7 6 5 4 3 2 1

Library of Congress Cataloging-in-Publication Data

Names: Hopper, Ada, author. | Ricks, Sam, illustrator. Title: Robots rule the school / by Ada Hopper ; illustrated by Sam Ricks. Description: First Little Simon paperback edition. | New York : Little Simon, 2016. | Series: The DATA set ; #4 | Summary: Mrs. Bell challenges her science students to invent their own robots but when they start malfunctioning it becomes up to the DATA Set to deprogram the machines before an army of robots take over the school. Identifiers: LCCN 2015038091| ISBN 9781481463133 (hc) | ISBN 9781481463126 (pbk) | ISBN 9781481463140 (ebook) Subjects: | CYAC: Robots—Fiction. | Inventions—Fiction. | Clubs—Fiction. | BISAC: JUVENILE FICTION / Readers / Chapter Books. | JUVENILE FICTION / Action & Adventure / General. | JUVENILE FICTION / Science Fiction. Classification: LCC PZ7.1.H66 Ro 2016 | DDC [E]—dc23 LC record available at http://lccn.loc.gov/2015038091

CONTENTS

CHAPTER 1

The Future Is Now!

Giant robotic planes did loop-the-loops in the sky! Fireworks burst in the air! Mechanical arms clapped and cheered while a little boy hugged a robot puppy.

"Gee, Sprocket," the boy said. "The future is awesome!"

"Arf, arf!" said the robot puppy.

"That's right, Timmy," said an announcer. "The future *is* awesome. And the future is . . . NOW! . . . now . . . now . . . now. . . ."

The announcer's voice faded out as the DATA Set's science teacher, Mrs. Bell, turned off the Smart Board.

"And that," Mrs. Bell said, "leads

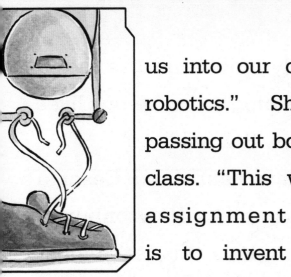 us into our chapter on robotics." She began passing out boxes to the class. "This week your assignment is to invent your own robots! These  kits have the gears and motors to get you started. Your robot can do anything. They can tie shoelaces.

 They can clean your room. They can even do your homework."

The students laughed.

"The only requirement is that it does something to make our lives better," Mrs. Bell said.

Gabe gave Laura and Cesar a big thumbs-up. As Newtonburg's resident whiz kids, this assignment was right up their alley!

Suddenly, a girl with straight blond hair and glasses shuffled

into the classroom. She handed Mrs. Bell a note.

"Ah, yes, it's so nice to meet you," said Mrs. Bell. "Class, welcome Olive Thompson. She was from Teslaville Prep, but now she will be joining us as a new student."

The class said hello, and Olive slowly waved back. Mrs. Bell directed Olive to an empty desk next to Cesar.

"Hi." Cesar held out his hand. "I'm Cesar."

Olive didn't answer.

"Like the emperor," Cesar joked about his name. "Or the salad."

Olive still didn't answer.

"*Ooooooookay,*" said Cesar.

He handed Olive a robot box kit. "So, uh, you used to go to Teslaville Prep? That's a tough school to get into. You must be pretty smart."

"Is that our assignment?" Olive asked abruptly. She pointed to an advanced mathematics problem on the whiteboard.

$$\frac{\partial v_i}{\partial t} + \sum_{j=1}^{3} v_j \frac{\partial v_i}{\partial x_j} \leq \frac{c}{(1+|x|)^k} \times \sqrt{n,y}$$

$$\int_{-\infty}^{\infty} e^{-x^2} dx \, (x,t) \, x^n e^{-x} dx = \,?$$

"No," said Cesar with a laugh. "That's the curve-buster board. Mrs. Bell puts up a super-stumper problem from the *National Science Academy Magazine* each week. If you solve it, you get an extra ten points on your next quiz. No one ever solves it, though—well, except Gabe that one time. . . ."

Before Cesar could finish, Olive walked over to the whiteboard. She erased a symbol in the equation and changed it to a new one before circling an answer.

"Yes, Olive, do you have a

question?" Mrs. Bell asked in surprise.

Suddenly Olive saw that the entire class-room was staring at her. Her cheeks flushed. "No, ma'am."

"May I ask what you are doing?" Mrs. Bell followed up.

"Solving the equation," said Olive. "The symbol was incorrect."

Mrs. Bell shook her head. "I copied that problem exactly." She pulled the magazine from her desk drawer. "I'm quite careful to . . ." The teacher trailed off. "Well, I'll be. You're right, Olive! The problem was incorrect—*and* you solved it. Gabe, it looks like you have a curve-buster buddy in class!"

Everyone's jaw dropped.

Especially Gabe's.

"Wow," said Cesar.

Olive *was* pretty smart.

Chapter 2

Robot Assistance

"I'm just saying, she was showing off a little, that's all," Gabe said.

He and his friends were walking home from school. They couldn't stop talking about Olive.

"You're just jealous because she figured out the answer instead of you," Laura teased.

"No," Gabe insisted. He paused. "Okay, well, maybe a little. I figured I'd have a chance to copy the problem down and work on it at home. I didn't realize she would solve it on the spot."

The friends looked across the street. There was Olive, walking home alone. She pushed her long

hair behind her ears and clutched her notebooks tightly.

"You sat next to her, Cesar," said Gabe. "What was she like?"

Cesar watched Olive turn a corner and shuffle out of sight. "Pretty," he said, distracted.

"Huh?" asked Gabe.

"Uh, pretty quiet," Cesar corrected himself. "But nice."

Gabe and Laura exchanged a glance.

"*Annnnyway*," said Laura. "Let's talk about robots. What are you guys making?"

At that, Cesar perked up. "I'm going to build a robot that stirs cake batter," he said excitedly.

Laura giggled. "That already exists. It's called a mixer."

"Yeah, but my robot is going to stir the batter *and* bake the cake at the same time! Super-fluffy

never-burned
cake with
no mess! I'll
name it the
Mix-and-Munch
Bot. Patent
pending."

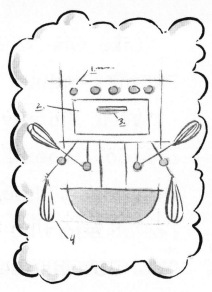

"Cool!" said Gabe. "What about

you, Laura?"

Laura thought
for a moment.
"Well, Mrs. Bell
said the robots
should make our
lives better."

"Like the Mix-and-Munch Bot. Patent pending," Cesar said.

"Well, I'm always searching for my tools when I'm working in the tree house," Laura continued. "So I'm going to build a Swiss-Army-Tool Bot that can store my tools and hand them to me when I need them."

"Sweet!" Gabe grinned.

"No, my idea is sweet," Cesar pointed out. "Her idea is more handy-dandy."

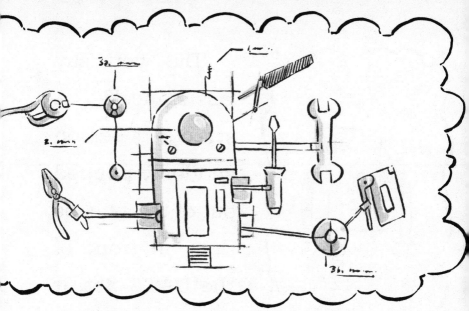

Gabe smiled. "Well, I'm going all-out artificial intelligence. I'm building a robotic classroom assistant! It will respond to voice commands and be able to learn so it can anticipate your next request. I think Mrs. Bell will be really impressed!"

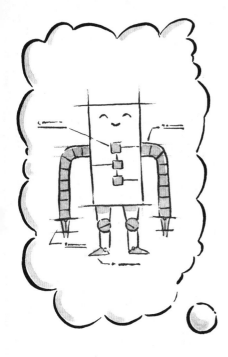

"Did you say 'assistance'?" A strange person suddenly popped out of the bushes right in front of the DATA Set. It was Dr. Bunsen, holding a metal detector.

"Ahh!" cried the kids.

"Dr. B.!" Gabe was startled.

"You really, *really* have to stop surprising us like that."

"Yes, quite!" agreed the doctor. "But until then, I believe I have just the robot assistance you three need. Follow me!"

Chapter 3

The Bunsen Stamp of Approval

"Mmmm-hmmm. Mmmm-hmmm."
Dr. Bunsen studied Gabe's, Laura's,
and Cesar's handiwork. The friends
were in his lab, using spare parts
to work on their robots.

"Impressive." The doctor stopped
in front of Cesar's Mix-and-Munch
Bot. It had a huge mixing bowl,

two robotic arms, and an oven for a head.

"It certainly *looks* like it can mix it up," observed the doctor. "But can it stand the heat in the kitchen?"

"Wait until you see it in action!" cried Cesar. He pressed a green button on the machine.

"It's munchin' time!" the robot announced. It used its robotic arms to plop ingredients into the bowl. Eggs, sugar, flour. Everything went in!

Whiiiirrrrrrrrrrr.

The mixer started spinning. It spun faster and faster. Cake batter flew everywhere!

"Whoa! That's not right," exclaimed Cesar.

He adjusted the dial. The mixer slowed . . . but the robot started flinging eggs instead!

"Bad Mix-and-Munch Bot!" Cesar furiously tried to shut it down.

Finally, the robot stopped.

Ding. Its oven timer went off. A sizzling black thing popped out, completely burned.

Cesar rubbed the back of his neck. "I guess it needs some adjustments."

"That's okay," Laura called

from across the lab. She was chasing her Swiss-Army-Tool Bot. "I'm not doing any better!"

Her robot was supposed to hand her tools, but it kept trying to use them instead!

"Stop, Bot!" Laura cried as it hammered yet another hole in the lab wall.

Meanwhile, every time Gabe gave his Classroom-Assistant Bot a command, it just kept hugging everything in sight.

"I—don't—get it," Gabe said as he wriggled free from its long arms. "It's built correctly, so why does it keep hugging me so much?"

"Maybe it thinks the assistance you need *is* a hug!" the doctor said.

"Hmmm, perhaps a fresh battery will help." He popped one of his specially designed Bunsen Infinity Batteries into the robot's power pack. Then the doctor swiveled the bot back around. "Now all

will be in order with a brand-new perspec-tive!"

The robot turned and focused on a messy pile

of paper. "Organization program activated," it said, stacking the papers neatly.

Gabe smiled. "Wow! Thanks, Dr. B.!"

"Say, a new perspective," Laura said thoughtfully. "That gives me an idea." Quickly, she rewired her bot so it thought the tools would work only if *she* used them. Instead of using the hammer itself, it finally handed it to Laura.

"It worked!" she cheered.

"And maybe my bot is going into overdrive because I programmed it to make cakes in half the time," said Cesar. "But really, all it needs to do is mix and bake simultaneously."

With a few adjustments, Cesar's robot finally worked!

"Excellent!" Dr. Bunsen clapped his hands. "I couldn't be prouder of you three. Your inventions each receive my Bunsen stamp of approval!"

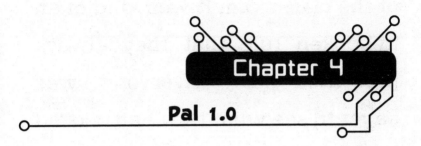

Chapter 4

Pal 1.0

That Friday all of the students presented their robots. Some had built simple inventions, like Cole's lever that could lift things. Others had built crazy contraptions, like a robot toilet flusher!

"Very good work, everyone," Mrs. Bell said. "Last but not least, we have Gabe, Laura, and Cesar."

The DATA Set went to the front of the classroom. It was kind of an unspoken rule that they always presented last. Everyone was eager to see what they had cooked up this time!

Laura went first. "Need a hand around the house? Swiss-Army-Tool Bot is your guy!" With a tap of Laura's remote control, Swiss-Army-Tool Bot opened a panel on the front of its body, revealing dozens of gadgets tucked inside.

"Oooooh," said the class.

"Or how about help tidying up the classroom?" Gabe said proudly. "Classroom-Assistant Bot, activate program 'Teacher's Aide.'"

Gabe's bot whirred to life! It stacked papers and wiped the Smart Board clean before handing Mrs. Bell a cup of coffee.

"You know what goes good with coffee?" Cesar piped up. "Cake!"

In no time flat, his Mix-and-Munch Bot mixed and baked cupcakes for the entire class!

"Cake for you! Cake for me! Cake for everyone!" cried Cesar.

"Hooray!" cheered the class.

"Nicely done," said Mrs. Bell. "I'm very impressed. I'd say you've all earned a relaxing homework-free weekend."

The kids were so excited, no one noticed the shy hand raised at the back of the class.

"Um, Mrs. Bell," said Olive. "I still have my robot to present."

"Oh my goodness!" Mrs. Bell gasped. "I'm so sorry, Olive. Please, come on up!"

Cesar watched Olive head to the front of the classroom.

He felt bad that she had to go after the DATA Set's high-tech robots.

Olive cleared her throat. She held up what looked like an alarm clock with a speaker.

"Did you make a clock?" Cesar asked helpfully.

Suddenly, two robotic eyes popped up from the top of her bot!

"Hello," the robot announced. "I am PAL 1.0, a virtual friend. I am programmed to play more than one hundred games and learn as I go."

"Wow," said the class.

"You made an AI robot, too?" Gabe asked, stunned.

Olive nodded with a small smile.

"Cool!" exclaimed Cesar. "Do you know any jokes, Pal 1.0?"

"What did the computer like to eat? Microchips and dip."

Everyone laughed!

"How about trivia?" asked Laura. "Who invented windshield wipers?"

"Mary Anderson in 1905."

Olive's robot was really cool!

"Oh, I've got one," said Cole. "Can you play tag?"

Pal 1.0 paused and whirred. "Recalculating, recalculating."

Olive frowned. "I'm sorry, Mrs. Bell. My robot seems to be broken."

"That's perfectly all right," said Mrs. Bell. "Your virtual friend would make many people's lives better. Great work!"

Chapter 5

Science Buddies

After science class, it was time for lunch. Cesar joined his friends at their usual table.

Suddenly, something caught his eye. Olive was sitting all by herself.

"Hey, guys," Cesar asked. "Should we go sit with Olive?"

Gabe frowned. "Really? She

keeps stealing my thunder."

"You mean because she built an AI robot?" Laura asked. "She didn't know that you made one too."

"Still." Gabe seemed uncertain. He actually did feel a little jealous of her robot and of how quickly she'd

answered the curve-buster math question. "I don't know. Do you guys want to sit with her?"

Cesar took a bite of his sandwich and glanced over at Olive. "She just seems lonely. And we're the DATA Set. Don't we help people?"

Gabe sighed. "I guess you're right."

Olive looked up in surprise when the friends approached her.

"Can we join you?" Cesar asked.

"Sure!" Olive scooched over so they could sit. "You're Cesar, right? Like the salad."

"Yeah!" Cesar couldn't believe she remembered the joke.

"And Gabe and Laura?" Olive said. "I really liked your robots."

"Thanks!" said Laura.

"We're pretty into science," Cesar added. "Kids around school

58

call us the DATA Set."

"That's cool." Olive smiled. "Your robots were programmed really well. Not like mine, which was all buggy."

Gabe raised his eyebrows. "That's not true. Your robot was super advanced."

"Besides, our bots had loads of problems in the beginning," added Cesar.

"Like what?" asked Olive.

"Well, for starters," said Gabe, "mine kept hugging everything."

"And mine threw eggs everywhere!" Cesar exclaimed.

Olive giggled. "I used to joke with my friends in Teslaville about invention mistakes all the time." She looked down. "I miss

them. I don't know anyone here, and I get so nervous."

"We'll be your new friends," Cesar offered eagerly. "You can hang out with us."

"Really?" Olive asked.

Cesar and Laura looked to Gabe. He nodded. "Of course."

The four kids chatted while they ate their lunch. It was nice having a new science buddy!

Suddenly, a voice came over the loudspeaker.

"All students report back to your classrooms."

Everyone filed out of the cafeteria. But when the kids reached their classroom, Mrs. Bell wasn't there.

"That's weird." Laura looked around. Something felt . . . off.

"Yeah," said Gabe. "Did you guys see any teachers as we came back?"

"And where did all our robots go?" Cesar asked, suddenly

alarmed. "My Mix-and-Munch Bot is missing!"

In fact, all the robots had disappeared!

Just then the classroom door opened.

Whirrrr! Bzzzzzt! Bzzzzzrrrrrr!

It was Gabe's robot . . . but it had been modified! New parts stuck out all over the place, and Olive's Pal 1.0 was on top as its head!

MUST CATCH ALL STUDENTS!

65

Chapter 6

Robot Mayhem

More robots piled in through the classroom door! Kids scattered in every direction to avoid getting caught!

"Yikes!" Cesar cried. "Let's get out of here!" He led Olive and the DATA Set out a side door and into the music wing of the school. They fled down the hall and came face-to-face with Cole's Lever-Bot!

It had been modified, too, and now had a trombone as a head!

"*Doo dee doo!*" the Trombone-Lever-Bot sounded.

"It's calling for backup!" Laura realized.

"Not if I can help it!" Cesar grabbed a cymbal from the music rack and used it as a shield to power past the robot. Its trombone head spun around!

"Wahhh, wahhh, wahhhhhh."
It played a sad slapstick tune as
the kids escaped.

"Quick! Let's go in here!" Laura
cried. The friends dashed inside
the empty library.

"I think we've lost them." Gabe
panted.

"How did the robots come to
life?" Cesar asked.

"And why are they all modified?"
Laura added.

"Shhhhh."

The shushing noise had come from behind them! The friends whipped around and saw the librarian, Mr. Paige, sitting at the front desk. His back was to them, but his Einsteinish-gray hair stuck out from over his typical argyle sweater.

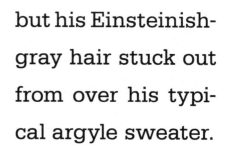

"It's Mr. Paige!" Cesar cried, rushing forward. "Help! Robots are taking over the school!"

"Shhhhhh," the librarian said again, not turning.

Gabe grabbed Cesar's arm. "Um, Mr. Paige?" Gabe asked warily.

The librarian's head suddenly swiveled around. It wasn't Mr. Paige at all! It was another robot wearing a sleeveless sweater and a gray mop as a wig!

"Ahhhhh!" The kids screamed and

raced into the book stacks. They ran back, back, back, ducking down in the darkest corner they could find.

Luckily, the robot librarian seemed more interested in shelving books than in catching them.

"Is this normal for your school?" Olive whispered.

"No," said Cesar. "Well, not super normal, anyway. But usually crazy stuff like this only happens when Dr. B. is around."

"Who's Dr. B.?" Olive asked.

"We'll tell you later," said Laura. "Right now we need to get help. Someone has reprogrammed all the robots to catch the students. And they are building new robots too, from the looks of it."

"We should try to get to an exit," Gabe said. "The police station isn't too far away. They can help us."

"Or we could get Dr. B.!" said Cesar. "He'll know what to do!"

Suddenly, the library doors banged and rattled.

"STUDENTS DETECTED! MUST CATCH ALL STUDENTS!"

The doors busted open! Dozens

of robots crashed through!

"We're trapped!" yelped Olive.

But before the robots could reach the book stacks, the librarian robot blocked their path.

"SHHHHH! SHHHH! SHHHH!"

"Now's our chance!" Gabe said urgently.

The friends crept along the back wall and zipped out before the robots spotted them. They raced

away as the *shush*ing sound of the librarian robot faded behind them.

Chapter 7

It's Munchin' Time

The DATA Set and Olive sneaked into the cafeteria. They could reach the emergency exit from there. All the lights were off, but there didn't seem to be any robots.

"I usually love the cafeteria," Cesar whispered. "But in the dark, it looks scary, in a yummy way."

"Do you think the robots caught all the other students?" Laura asked.

"I don't know," said Gabe, worried.

The friends tiptoed as quickly as they could.

"Who do you think is behind this?" Laura asked.

"Maybe the robots are," said Olive.

Laura looked at her. "What do you mean?"

"If someone were controlling the bots, wouldn't we have seen them?" Olive pointed out. "It's like the robots are acting on their own. Like they've gotten smarter."

"Is that even possible?" asked Gabe. "I know your bot and mine were AI. But all the others were just motors and gears."

"Maybe our bots worked together to modify the others," Olive said.

Gabe shook his head. "I programmed my robot to be smart, but not *that* smart. There's no way it had the power to lead a robot rebellion!"

Suddenly, a *whirring* noise echoed

from the cafeteria kitchen. It grew louder.

"I think quiet time is over!" exclaimed Cesar. "Run!"

The kids bolted to the exit doors and tried to tug them open. They

were locked with chains!

"No! Who would ever *lock up* the emergency exit!" Cesar exclaimed. "Who?"

An enormous robot wheeled out from the kitchen. It lifted its giant mixer and rotated it slowly.

Cesar smacked his head. "You have *got* to be kidding me. BAD Mix-and-Munch Bot!"

WHIRRRRRRRRRR! The mixer spun faster! "PREHEATING OVEN MODE," it announced in its robotic voice.

"Don't make it angry, Cesar!" Laura cried. "Just run!"

The friends sprinted back across the cafeteria. "I don't want to be an ingredient!" Cesar yelled as the Mix-and-Munch Bot whirred at their heels.

"This way!" Gabe banged open a hall door into the boys' room and the friends darted through. The Mix-and-Munch Bot was too wide to follow. It *buzzed* angrily!

"Hurry!" Gabe exclaimed.

Inside the friends found a door that connected to the gym locker room.

"Phew," said Olive as the friends crept into the gym. "That was close—eeeeeek!" she yelped. Dozens of large figures loomed there.

"It's gymnastics equipment, not robots." Cesar said

Olive breathed a sigh of relief. Cesar was right. Vaults, uneven bars, and balance beams were set up everywhere.

"Now what?" asked Laura. "What if all the exits are locked?"

"We have to keep trying until we find a way out," Gabe said, determined. "We may be the school's only hope. We have to get help."

Just then a scruffy-haired shadow stepped toward the kids. "Did someone say 'help'?"

Chapter 8

Save the School!

Gabe couldn't believe his eyes. It was Dr. Bunsen! "Dr. B., you *really* have to stop doing that." He broke into a huge grin. "But boy are we glad to see you!"

"As am I, my young DATA Set!" the doctor replied. He looked at Olive. "And the DATA Set's young friend."

"Oh, how rude of me. Dr. B., this is Olive," said Cesar.

"Are you here to stop the bots?" Laura asked the doctor hopefully.

"Er, not exactly," Dr. B. said. "But your question does make me worry."

"Robots have taken over the school." Cesar acted out their day.

"Somehow all of our robots were reprogrammed to capture the school," Gabe added.

"We think they've gotten smarter," said Laura.

The doctor scratched his head. "Ah, yes. Well, you may have me to thank for that. That's why I came. You see, when I put the Bunsen

Infinity Battery in your robot, Gabe, I may have accidently put an Artificial Intelligence Booster Power Pack in it instead."

"A what?" asked Gabe.

Cesar looked to Olive. "See? This is what I meant."

The doctor shrugged. "My Infinity Battery and AI Booster do tend to look the same. I have a note on my 'to do' list to mark them properly. Oh, well, you know how it is. Busy and all."

Olive turned to Gabe. "So *that's* how your bot got smarter."

Gabe nodded. "Smart enough to combine with Pal 1.0 and build all the other bots."

"Did they really? Oh, how excellent!" The doctor clapped his hands. "Well, not excellent that they've taken over the school. But quite exciting that my AI Booster is working so well!"

"Can we stop them?" asked Gabe.

"Of course," said Bunsen. You just need to—"

Suddenly, the gymnasium doors burst open!

It was Laura's Swiss-Army-Tool Bot, brandishing lassos made from tape measures!

"Hold that thought, Dr. B.!" exclaimed Gabe.

The friends bounced off of the vaults and swung over balance beams!

"Wow." Cesar watched Olive somersault over a vault. She was good at gymnastics, *too*?

But it was no use. The Swiss-Army-Tool Bot had cornered them in the gym locker room.

"Stop!" Laura stepped in front of her robot. "Remember what you're programmed to do! You're supposed to hand *me* the tools! They won't work without me."

The robot paused, confused. It couldn't decide if it should follow its old programming or its new programming.

Suddenly, the wall behind the DATA Set crashed open! It was Cole's Lever-Bot, but now it had two enormous mechanical arms!

It grabbed Dr. Bunsen and whizzed off!

"Dr. B.!" the kids cried.

Laura's Swiss-Army-Tool Bot zipped after it, still confused. But the friends weren't fast enough to rescue Dr. Bunsen.

"Remove the power pack and save the school!" the doctor cried before disappearing down the hall in the robot's clutches.

Chapter 9

Operation: Tag

"It's up to us now," said Gabe. "We have to rescue Dr. B. and the others."

"You guys are free?" a nervous voice whispered. "I thought I was the only one."

It was Cole! He had been hiding under a locker-room bench.

"Cole!" exclaimed Laura. "Are you okay?"

He nodded. "I hid when the robots attacked. They missed me."

"What happened to everyone else?" Gabe asked.

"The robots took everyone to the teachers' lounge," Cole said. "They even have a leader—Olive, somehow your bot combined with Gabe's

and gave orders to 'catch all the students' and 'win the game.'"

"Win the game. . . ." Olive smiled. She had figured out the robot's plan. "Of course! Cole asked my robot to play tag. Pal 1.0 is playing tag!"

"But it couldn't complete the

request on its own," Gabe realized. "It needed my bot's assistance to help gather and organize the students."

"And with the

AI Power Pack . . . ," said Laura.

"It built all the bots to play tag too," finished Cesar.

The friends were relieved to finally understand what was going on at their school!

"So how do we get close enough to unplug that power pack?" asked Laura.

A smile crossed Gabe's face. "We need to play tag."

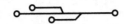

"This way!" Laura and Cole sprinted down a hallway. "Those robots won't catch us!"

"Humans rule! Robots drool!" yelled Gabe from up ahead.

Robots *whirr*ed and *buzz*ed angrily as they moved out from classroom doors. There were bots of all shapes and sizes—modified inventions and even more newly built ones. And at the front of the pack was Pal 1.0 on top of Gabe's Classroom-Assistant Bot.

Gabe, Laura, and Cole backed against the lockers. This didn't look good.

"ROBOTS WIN." Pal 1.0's robot eyes popped up, flashing red. "PROGRAM SCHOOL TAG: COMPLETE. ALL STUDENTS CAPTURED. NOW ROBOTS MUST CAPTURE ENTIRE TOWN!"

"That's what you think," Gabe said. "Hit it!"

Suddenly, Cesar and Olive jumped down from a hiding spot on top of the lockers! Together they landed on Cole's Lever-Bot. The lever shot up . . . smacking right into Pal 1.0's AI Booster Power Pack and sending it flying!

"NO!" cried Pal 1.0. "MUST . . . CAPTure . . . all . . . stuuuuuuu . . ."

The voice went silent as the red light faded from Pal 1.0's eyes. All of the other bots shut down! Olive stepped forward to catch her bot as it toppled from Gabe's Classroom Assistant.

Pal 1.0's eyes blinked back to the color green. "Hello," it said to Olive in its normal voice. "I am Pal 1.0, a robot friend. Shall we play a game?"

"No thanks," Olive said. "I think we're all gamed out."

Chapter 10

The DATA Set 2.0

The DATA Set, Cole, and Olive burst into the teachers' lounge.

"Dr. B.! Mrs. Bell! Please say you are all o- . . . kay?"

"Oh, there you guys are!" said a student named Chaz as he buzzed by on an electric scooter.

"What took you so long?" asked

another classmate named Heather. She was playing Ping-Pong against Mrs. Bell.

The DATA Set couldn't believe their eyes. All the students and teachers were packed into an enormous game room! Pinball machines lined the walls. Principal Stevens was making espresso shots at a bar.

There was even an air hockey table!

Gabe blinked. "Did the robots do this?"

"No," said Mrs. Bell as she served the ball in a game of Ping-Pong. "Our lounge was always this way."

"When the robots started acting up, they brought us here," said Chaz as he made another scooter lap.

"We were going to escape," said the real librarian, Mr. Paige. He shot a basketball into a hoop that hung on the wall. "But we figured the robots would run out of batteries sooner or later. So we decided to take the rest of the afternoon off to have fun."

Cesar was in shock. "But I—I don't—HOW DID WE NOT KNOW ABOUT THIS?"

"Oh, there you are!" Dr. Bunsen ran up to the kids. He was wearing a virtual reality gaming helmet. "Did you end up saving the school?"

"Did you—did we—" Cesar sputtered.

Olive patted Cesar's shoulder. "We sure did."

While the students and teachers continued to play in the teachers' lounge, Laura and Olive quickly powered up Laura's Swiss-Army-Tool Bot to help repair the damage to the school. Dr. B. helped too.

"So, my young DATA Set," said the doctor. "Now that you have all earned A's on your robot projects, destroyed the school, *and* saved the school, what will you do this weekend?"

Cesar shrugged. "I don't know. Probably relax. It's not like we have a SECRET GAME ROOM TO

SNEAK OFF TO OR ANYTHING!" he shouted back down the hallway toward the teachers' lounge.

"But we do have Laura's super-awesome tree house, which is just as good," said Gabe.

"A super-awesome tree house?" asked Olive. "I'd like to see that."

The DATA Set exchanged glances.

"I'm afraid only members of the DATA Set are allowed inside," said Laura.

"You should come check it out," Gabe said with a grin.

Olive broke into a huge smile. "Do you mean it?"

Cesar tossed a spare

robot part into the air and caught it. He winked. "When it comes to officially welcoming new members of the DATA Set, we never play games."

CHECK OUT THE NEXT DATA SET ADVENTURE!

Mmmmm. I taste cranberry and pumpkin . . . ," Cesar said as he took another gulp of juice. "With a hint of turkey gravy."

"No way. Something's wrong with your taste buds," said Laura. "It tastes like peach cobbler."

"You're both wrong," said Gabriel.

"This is totally a banana milk shake."

"Oh, excellent!" Dr. Gustav Bunsen clapped his hands. "My Juice-o-Tronic 2000 works perfectly!"

Gabe, Laura, and Cesar were in Dr. Bunsen's laboratory, helping him test his newest invention, when they should have been doing their homework. But Dr. Bunsen insisted that they try his perfect "pick-me-up" drinks first to boost their energy.

It was going to be a busy day.

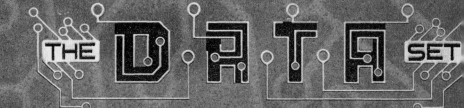

THE DATA SET

FOR MORE DANGER! ACTION! TROUBLE! ADVENTURE!

Visit thedatasetbooks.cor